No part of this book may be reproduced or transmitted in any form or by any means, electronic or mechanical, including photocopying, recording, or stored in a retrieval system or otherwise, without the written permission from the publisher. For information regarding permission, write to Kia Harris Juniors, an imprint of Kia Harris, LLC dba KH Publishers, 88 Route 17M, STE 1012, Harriman, NY 10926.

www.iamkiaharris.com

ISBN 978-1-953237-03-3

Text and illustrations copyright ©2020 by Qiana Davis. All rights reserved.
Published by Kia Harris Juniors, an imprint of Kia Harris, LLC dba KH Publishers.

The publisher does not have any control over and does not assume any responsibility for author or third-party websites or their content or any other media, social or othewr.

Printed in the U.S.A.

First Paperback Edition, December 2020

To my 3-heartbeats Elijah, Keyshawn, and Brandon, never stop dreaming! Remember, you can do all things through Christ that strengthens you.

To the love of my life Wendel, thank you for loving me always and in all ways.

To the children of Elizabeth Public Schools, I am thankful, grateful, and blessed to be your teacher. You have, and will always be my "Why."

Love is friends.

How do you show love to your friends?

Love is pizza.

What do you love to eat?

Why is it important to love your family?

Love is hugs.

Who gives you the best hugs?

Love is laughter.

Who makes you laugh?

Love is learning.

If you were the teacher, what would you teach the class?

Love is kind.

How did you show kindness today?

Love is me
Love is you
Love is in everything we do!

From the top of my head

To the soles of my feet

I LOVE every part of me!

How do you show love to your friends?

What do you love to eat?

Why is it important to love your family?

Who gives you the best hugs?

Who makes you laugh?

If you were the teacher, what would you teach the class?

How did you show kindness today?

CPSIA information can be obtained
at www.ICGtesting.com
Printed in the USA
LVHW072309230321
682295LV00002B/22